WHY DO PEOPLE EAT?

Kate Needham

Designed by Lindy Dark and Non Figg

Illustrated by Annabel Spenceley and Kuo Kang Chen

Consultants: Dr Frank Slattery and Valerie Micheau

CONTENTS

Why do you need food?

Your body is like a big machine that is always working. Even when you are asleep your heart is beating, your lungs are breathing and your brain is working. Food is the fuel which keeps all these things going. Without it you would slow down and eventually grind to a halt.

A bar of chocolate gives you enough energy to walk for an hour.

People need food just as cars need gasoline.

An apple gives you enough energy to cycle for six minutes.

Growing big and strong

People sometimes say you have to eat things to grow big and strong. This is true because your whole body is made from good things in the food you eat.

Until you are about 18 your body is growing all the time.

Measure yourself each month to see how quickly you grow.

Sometimes when you haven't eaten you feel weak. This is because your body is running out of energy.

Children who don't get enough food stop growing. They become thin and weak and become ill more easily.

Too much

If you eat more food than your body needs you store it as fat. This makes you heavy and slows you down.

Some people want to be big and heavy so they overeat on purpose. For example Japanese sumo wrestlers need to be heavy to fight.

Sumo wrestlers look like this.

On the mend

The good things in the food you eat help your body make repairs if it gets damaged. They also help you get better when you are ill.

When you cut yourself, the food you eat helps your body mend quickly.

Water

Water is what keeps your body moist and makes your blood flow around. Without it your body would dry out and stop working.

You can last several weeks without food but only a few days without water.

Loading and unloading bread from an oven is hot, thirsty work.

Shipwrecked sailors more often die of thirst than hunger, since they can't drink seawater.

People who work in hot places, such as a baker, need to drink more because they lose water when they sweat.

3

What is food made of?

Everything you eat is made up of lots of different things called nutrients. These are the good things that keep your body going. Proteins, fats and carbohydrates are all nutrients. Each one helps your body do a special job.

Protein

Proteins are like building blocks. Your body uses them to grow and repair itself. Different kinds of proteins help build up each part of your body.

Proteins build up muscles and make your hair grow.

Teenagers use up lots of proteins because they are growing fast.

Pregnant women need extra protein to help their baby grow.

A mother's milk has special proteins in it.

Meat, eggs, fish and cheese have lots of protein.

4

Carbohydrates

Carbohydrates give you energy. You need energy for everything you do such as running around, talking, thinking, even reading this book.

You get lots of energy from sweet things but it doesn't last very long. The energy you get from pasta, cereal or bread is better because it lasts longer.

Climbers often carry a bar of chocolate in case they need extra energy in an emergency.

Athletic people need carbohydrates for extra energy.

Bread, cereal, pasta and cakes have lots of carbohydrates.

Fat

Fat also gives you energy but unless your body needs it right away, it is stored in a layer around your body. This acts like an extra piece of clothing helping to keep you warm and protect you.

Butter, margarine and oil are almost all fat.

Fat stored on your bottom makes it more comfortable to sit on, like a little cushion.

What else is in food?

The food you eat also has tiny amounts of nutrients called vitamins and minerals which you need.

What do vitamins do?

Vitamins are like little workers which help other nutrients to do their jobs. There are about 20 different kinds. Most are named after letters of the alphabet.

The chart opposite shows what some vitamins do and where you find them.

A

Vitamin A helps you see in the dark.

You find it in egg yolks, liver, homogenized milk and carrots.

B

There are lots of kinds of B vitamins, each with a different job.

Cereals, dairy products and meat have B vitamins.

C

Vitamin C is good for health and body repairs.

You find it in fresh fruit and vegetables.

D

Vitamin D helps make your bones and teeth strong.

You get it from eggs, fish and butter.

Sailors used to get scurvy – a disease which stops wounds from healing. This is because they were at sea for months without any fresh vegetables or fruit and so no vitamin C.

Your body can make vitamin D itself using sunlight. People who live in less sunny countries need extra vitamin D from their food.

What are minerals?

Minerals are nutrients that plants get from soil and pass on to you. You need about 15 different ones such as salt, calcium and iron.

Water has lots of minerals in it.

Liver, meat and spinach have tiny amounts of iron in them which you need for your blood.

Milk, cheese and yogurt have calcium in them which makes your teeth and bones strong.

What is fiber?

Fiber is the tough bit of food that you don't digest. It helps carry food through you and takes waste out the other end.

Brown bread, cereals and vegetables have lots of fiber.

If you don't eat enough fiber you get constipated – this is when you can't go to the toilet for ages.

What do you eat?

Write down everything you ate and drank in your last main meal. Then see if you can find out which nutrients each thing had. Use the last two pages for help.

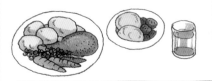

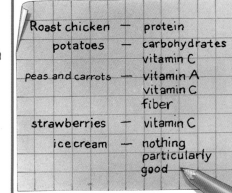

Roast chicken	—	protein
potatoes	—	carbohydrates vitamin C
peas and carrots	—	vitamin A vitamin C fiber
strawberries	—	vitamin C
ice cream	—	nothing particularly good

How many good things did you eat? Were there any you didn't get any of? Some things you eat, such as ice cream, may not have anything particularly good in them, see page 16.

Where does food go?

When you eat, your food starts a long journey through your body which takes about three days. It travels through a tube called the alimentary canal which starts at your mouth and finishes at your bottom.

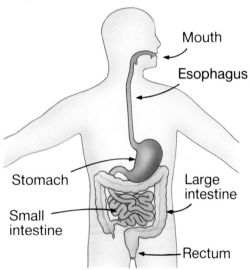

Mouth

Esophagus

Stomach

Large intestine

Small intestine

Rectum

On the way, different parts of your body work on the food and add juices with chemicals in them. This breaks food into microscopically small pieces that can go into your blood. This journey is called digestion.

Food's journey

The road in this picture is like the alimentary canal, and the men show what happens to your food.

Your mouth

These men are like your teeth, cutting food into tiny pieces.

The water is like saliva. It makes food soft and mushy.

Your tongue rolls the food into a ball and pushes it into your esophagus, like these men with brooms.

Esophagus

Then you swallow, and food is carried off from your mouth to continue its journey.

How long to chew?

The smaller food gets in your mouth, the easier it is for your stomach to work on. Tough meat or food with lots of fiber needs more chewing.

Eat a mouthful of apple. Then eat one of cheese.

See how many times you chew each one before you swallow?

What makes you choke?

Your esophagus is next to your windpipe (the pipe you breathe through). When you swallow, your windpipe closes to stop food from going into it.

If it doesn't close in time your food might go down the wrong way. This makes you choke which usually sends the food back up.

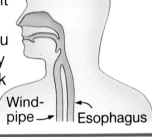

Wind-pipe → | Esophagus

Your stomach

To your intestines

In your body, it goes down a tube called your esophagus. This delivers food to your stomach by squeezing it along.

Your stomach is like a big mixing machine. It churns your food up until it is like soup.

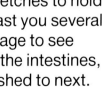

Your stomach stretches to hold enough food to last you several hours. Turn the page to see what happens in the intestines, where food is pushed to next.

Good things and waste

After about three hours, the soupy mixture in your stomach moves on to your intestines. There, all the good things in food are taken into the blood. The way it happens is called absorption. Waste moves on to leave your body. This is the longest part of food's journey.

How goodness is absorbed

The walls of your small intestine are so thin that the nutrients in your food can pass through them.

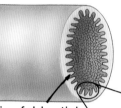

The nutrients go into your blood and are carried around your body.

Tiny folds stick out of the walls of the small intestine.

Blood flows all around the folds, ready to carry off nutrients.

Your small intestine

First the food arrives in your small intestine. This isn't really small at all, as it's a long tube all curled up.

As the soupy mixture passes through it, more juices are added. Then nutrients are absorbed into your blood (the man's sign tells them to stay). The rest goes into your large intestine (the man's sign tells them they must go).

Your large intestine

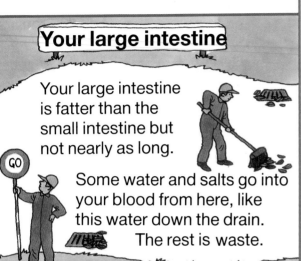

Your large intestine is fatter than the small intestine but not nearly as long.

Some water and salts go into your blood from here, like this water down the drain. The rest is waste.

Getting rid of waste

Waste from your large intestine is solid. It goes into your rectum and is pushed out through your bottom when you go to the toilet.

Waste water is turned into urine in your kidneys. It is stored in your bladder until you go to the toilet.

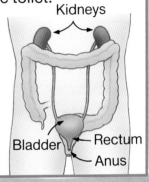

Kidneys

Bladder — Rectum

Anus

What makes you burp?

When you eat you often swallow air with your food. Sometimes your body sends the air back up through your mouth. This is a burp.

BURP!

Eating too fast makes you swallow lots of air and so you may burp.

Food poisoning

If you eat food that is bad, your body tries to get rid of it quickly.

Your stomach muscles may push it back up your esophagus. This is when you are sick.

It may rush through you and come out the other end as diarrhea.

11

Keeping food fresh

Your food is also food for tiny living things called microbes. These can make fresh food go bad after a few days. If you want food to keep, you have to stop microbes from getting in it first. They like moisture, warmth and air, so food kept in cold, dry places with no air lasts longer.

No air

Today, lots of food is vacuum-packed. This is when all the air is sucked out of the packet. Bottles and cans have no air either. Can you hear air rushing back in when you open them?

VACUUM-PACKED PEANUTS

Keeping food cold

Cooling food slows microbes down; freezing it stops them altogether. Today, food can be kept in refrigerators or freezers until it is needed.

Cold cellars have been used to keep food for centuries.

The cold does not kill microbes, so you still have to eat food quickly when you defrost it.

Drying food

Drying food gets rid of all the moisture so microbes can't multiply.

Grapes are dried to make raisins, sultanas and currants.

Today, food can be freeze-dried. This is when it is frozen and dried at the same time to get rid of moisture. You add water when you eat it.

Astronauts use freeze-dried food as it's light and takes little room.

Heating food

Cooking, sterilization and pasteurization are all ways of killing microbes by heat.

Sterilized food is heated to a very high temperature to kill all the microbes. It lasts a long time.

Sugar in jam
Vinegar in pickles
Salt in bacon

Food in cans and bottles is sterilized.

Preservatives:
Benzoic acid
(E210)

Preservatives

Preservatives are chemicals that make food last. Natural ones like sugar, vinegar and salt, have been used for centuries.

Look at labels on cans to see what other chemicals are used as preservatives today.

Pasteurized milk is heated enough to kill dangerous microbes. It lasts a few days.

Before pasteurization, cows were led around towns and milked on the doorstep.

Food you store loses some nutrients, particularly vitamins, so it is better to eat fresh food.

Food from far away

These days food can be kept fresh for so long that shops have exotic fruits from all over the world. They travel in specially refrigerated ships.

Next time you go to a supermarket, see if it says where the fruit comes from on the shelves.

Pineapple
Mangoes
Banana   Passion fruit
Lychees

What makes you hungry?

When your body needs food, it sends a message to your brain to say so. Then you look around to find something to eat.

Sometimes, when you see or smell food you like, it can make you feel hungry even though your body doesn't need food.

Nose smells food

The smell of food tells you if it is good or bad and if you like it or not.

Eyes see food

Even thinking about food can make you feel hungry.

Stomach is empty

What makes your mouth water?

When you see or smell food you like, your body gets ready to eat. You may feel water in your mouth. This is saliva, the juice your mouth makes to help mix your food.

Saliva dripping from a dog's mouth means that he is ready to eat.

Tummy rumbles

Sometimes, when your stomach is getting ready for food, it makes a rumbling noise. The sound you can hear is air and digestive juices being pushed around inside.

Tasting food

You can tell what food you do and don't like by the taste of it. Your tongue is what you mainly use to taste food. It is covered with lots of tiny bumps called taste buds.

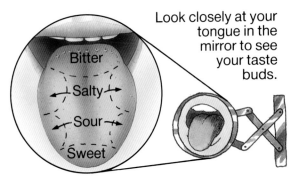

Look closely at your tongue in the mirror to see your taste buds.

There are four types of taste buds. Each tells a different kind of taste: salty, sweet, sour and bitter. They are on different parts of your tongue.

The smell of things helps you taste them as well. Try holding your nose when you eat. Can you taste your food?

Try this

Dip your finger in some salt. Put it on the tip of your tongue, then on the back and finally on the side. Which part can you taste it on most?

Do the same with sugar, lemon juice and coffee. Can you tell which kind of taste they are?

See if you can fill in a chart like the one below.

Food	Part of tongue	Taste
Salt	Back of side	
Sugar		sweet
Lemon		
Coffee		

Professional tasters

Some people can tell different tastes more easily than others. They may become professional wine- or tea-tasters.

15

Food that's bad for you

If you only ate your favorite food, your body wouldn't get all the good things it needs.

Some foods have very little goodness and can be bad for you if you eat too much of them.

Sweet things

Sugar is what makes things sweet. It is a carbohydrate so it gives you energy, but too much of it makes you fat. It also makes your teeth rot.

The more sweet things you eat, the more fillings you are likely to have at the dentist's.

Fatty food

Food that is fried, such as a burger, has lots of extra fat. It makes you feel full so you may not eat other things that are good for you.

Having extra fat is like carrying heavy bags. Your body and heart have to work harder to carry the weight.

What is junk food?

Food that has mostly bad things and very few good things in it is called junk food.

Candy and soft drinks are nearly all sugar.

Ice creams, milk shakes and cookies are mostly fat and sugar.

Fast food is often fried and so has extra fat.

What is a food allergy?

Some people feel bad every time they eat a certain kind of food. They may get a headache or a rash or be sick. This is called a food allergy.

One person's favorite food can make another person feel really ill.

Many people are allergic to fish, eggs, strawberries or shellfish.

Special problems with food

Some people's bodies can't store sugar so they can only eat a little of it. Some need injections to help their body use sugar properly. This problem is called diabetes.

Some chocolate is made without sugar so that people with diabetes can enjoy it, too.

Other people's bodies don't like gluten – a protein in wheat. They can't eat things with wheat or wheat flour in them. This problem is called celiac disease.

Can you guess which things in this picture have wheat in them? The answer is at the bottom of page 18.

Religion

Some people don't eat certain kinds of food because their religion says they shouldn't. Muslims and Jews don't eat pork, for example.

Where does food come from?

Almost everything you eat comes from a living thing: either a plant or an animal.

Plants make their own food, using energy from the sun. Animals eat plants or other animals. So do people. The way one thing eats another is called a food chain.

Energy from the sun.

You get energy from cow's milk.

Energy goes from the grass to the cow.

Bread and cereals come from corn.

Beef, cheese and milk come from cows.

In this picture, do you know where all the picnic food comes from? Can you find out what the food chain of the egg is? Turn to the bottom of page 20 for the answer.

Answer from page 17: All of them.

People who don't eat meat

People who choose not to eat any meat are called vegetarians. Some don't like the taste of meat. Others don't like to kill animals and think the way they are kept is cruel.

Some people don't eat anything at all that comes from animals. They are called vegans.

Vegans don't eat meat, fish, milk, eggs and cheese.

Vegetarians don't eat meat. Some don't eat fish.

Most people get most of the protein they need from meat, though there is some in plants. Vegetarians and vegans must take care to get enough protein.

How are animals kept?

For most farmers, the comfort of the animals is not as important as producing lots of food as cheaply as possible. This is because people usually buy cheaper food.

For example, hens usually stop laying eggs at night. But if they are kept in warm cages with the lights on, they lay for longer.

Hens that run around the farm are called free-range hens.

Hens kept in cages are called battery hens. They can lay about 270 eggs a year.

A free-range hen may only lay 80 eggs a year, so its eggs are more expensive.

19

Is there enough food?

If all the food in the
world was spread
evenly among all
the people,
everyone would
have enough to eat.
But it isn't like that.

In rich parts of the world like Europe,
North America and Australia, most
people get plenty to eat. Some eat
too much.

Families in rich countries
tend to be smaller so
there are fewer people
to share the food.

In poor parts of the world like Africa,
Southeast Asia and South America
people have a lot less to eat. Many
don't get enough.

Families in these
countries tend to be
larger so there are more
mouths to feed.

Other problems in poor countries

Without rain you cannot grow things.
Some African countries have had no
rain for several years and their
farmland is now desert.

If there is a war, land for growing food
may be destroyed. Often food from
other countries can't get through to
help feed people.

Answer from page 18: egg – chicken – corn.

What is malnutrition?

Malnutrition is when people don't get enough of the right nutrients. This means they catch diseases more easily.

In many poor countries people don't get enough protein. Children especially need protein to grow. Most protein comes from animals. They are expensive to keep so many people can't afford them.

What is a famine?

A famine is when there is so little food that people die. Often they die of diseases caused by malnutrition.

Who helps?

There are organizations in rich countries which send some food and help to places where there is famine.

Future food

If the population of the whole world keeps growing there won't be enough food for everyone, particularly meat, fish and eggs.

So scientists are busy searching for new kinds of food, especially plants with lots of protein.

Soya is a plant from China which has lots of protein. It can be made to look and taste like other food.

Some seaweeds are rich in protein. It grows all over the world but it is only eaten in a few countries, such as Japan, so far.

Around the world

People in different countries eat different things. This is because each part of the world has different plants and animals. This map shows you three main crops that grow in different parts of the world.

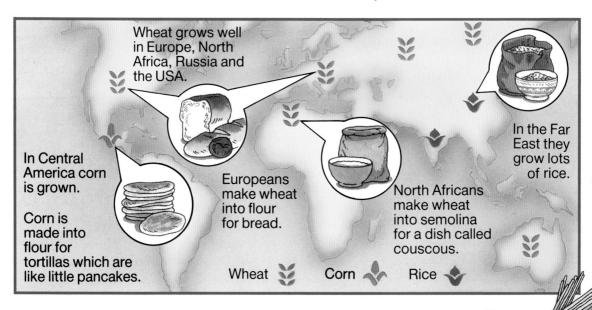

Wheat grows well in Europe, North Africa, Russia and the USA.

In Central America corn is grown.

Corn is made into flour for tortillas which are like little pancakes.

Europeans make wheat into flour for bread.

North Africans make wheat into semolina for a dish called couscous.

In the Far East they grow lots of rice.

Wheat   Corn   Rice

Food that has traveled

Lots of the food we eat every day was first found in distant countries by explorers.

Potatoes were discovered by the Spanish in South America in the 16th century.

Turkeys were also found by the Spanish, in Mexico.

Spices like cloves, pepper and cinnamon were carried back from the East in the Middle Ages.

Pasta was found in the Far East by the famous Italian explorer Marco Polo.

Unusual food

People in other countries eat all sorts of things that you may never have tried.

In some parts of the world people eat insects which have lots of protein in them.

On Chinese stalls like this one you can buy beetles, bats, snakes or even so-called 100 year-old eggs.

Insects are common food in many parts of Africa.

Ants are eaten in Colombia.

Grasshoppers are cooked and eaten in Mexico.

Ways to eat

In Western countries most people eat with a knife and fork.

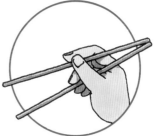

In countries in the Far East people use two wooden sticks called chopsticks.

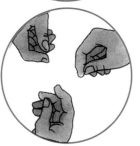

In India everyone eats from the same dish with one hand only, always the right hand.

Vacations abroad

If you go on vacation abroad, see if you notice any different things people eat and the way they eat them.

Index

First published in 1992. Usborne Publishing Ltd, Usborne House, 83-85 Saffron Hill, London EC1N 8RT, England. Copyright © 1992 Usborne Publishing Ltd.
First published in America in March 1993.